THE NILE FILES

Stories about Ancient Egypt

THE WOBBLY OBELISK

by Philip Wooderson

Illustrations by Andy Hammond

W
FRANKLIN WATTS
LONDON•SYDNEY

First published in 2001 by Franklin Watts
96 Leonard Street, London EC2A 4XD

Text © Philip Wooderson 2001
Illustrations © Andy Hammond 2001

The right of Philip Wooderson to be identified as
the Author of this Work has been asserted by
him in accordance with the Copyright, Designs
and Patents Act, 1988

Editor: Lesley Bilton
Designer: Jason Anscomb
Consultant: Dr Anne Millard, BA Hons, Dip Ed, PhD

A CIP catalogue record for this book
is available from the British Library

ISBN 0 7496 4189 4 (hbk)
0 7496 4370 6 (pbk)

Dewey Classification 932

Printed in Great Britain

CONTENTS

To: **Supadupa,**
High Priestess
The Temple at Hokus
Near Pokus

Topic: The New Obelisk

Get it up for the feast of Opet.
The Fearful Pharaoh will be coming to
honour the god Amen-Ra. You should stick
it in the courtyard, next to the obelisk for
Pharaoh's father - King Milksop.
Pharaoh has composed his own words
to go on the stone. So on the Great Day
you must tell him what a great poet he is!!!!

Pharaoh's Chief
Counsellor
Donut

"Just look how it catches the light," said Dad. He held up the precious gem that had come from Queen Hedbutt's death mask. "Amazing. Sheer poetry, Ptoni. Let's trade it and get a new boat. I'll call it *The Queen of the Nile*, and take rich nobs on cruises. We'll all have a wonderful time."

His crew didn't seem as keen.

"*You'll* have a wonderful time, chief . . ."

"While *we* slave away as usual without getting any wages . . ."

"Will anything ever change . . . ?"

"Yes, I've been thinking," Dad grinned, "now that I've got my priceless gem . . ."

"*Our* amethyst," grumbled one of the crew.

"Perhaps I should make a Will. Then you could sleep easy at nights, lads, knowing that if I pop off my son, Ptoni, will be my heir and he can pay you your wages. Right, where's my personal scribe? I'll need him to write down the details."

"Stupor's asleep, Dad," said Ptoni. "He's been at the beer again. And wouldn't it be better to get your Will written properly – by a priest at a temple?"

"Good thinking," said Dad, as he glanced across at a settlement on the far bank of the river Nile. "And very good timing, too."

Ptoni could see crowds of people unloading huge blocks of stone from several boats moored at a jetty. Behind them were tents and mud huts clustered round a much larger building.

"Here's the temple at Hokus," said Dad.
"I'll have my Will sorted by sunset."

CHAPTER 2
THERE'S A WAY

As soon as they stepped ashore, Dad and Ptoni set off for the temple.* Ptiddles, the ship's cat, padded behind them. Dad hailed a workman. "What's happening here, my good man?"

The man was chiselling hieroglyphics on the side of a long lump of stone. "Pharaoh's due to visit the temple for the Feast of Opet. He'll be here in two days' time and we've not got his new obelisk up yet."

* Find out more about temples on page 60

"What are you writing?" asked Ptoni.

"Search me. I can't read hieroglyphics. I'm only Skratch the Engraver. I just copy what I'm given." The worker showed them a dog-eared scroll. "Pharaoh wrote this – with his own hand."

"Ah, yes."
Dad pretended to
read it. "Surprisingly good.
But I'd better push on. I've got a legal matter
to sort out at the temple."

"Huh, you'll be lucky," said Skratch. He pointed out the entrance. It was blocked by a temple guard.

"Only priests and royal officials allowed in here," growled the guard.

"Well, I'm a part-time official," claimed Dad. "In fact, I've just solved a problem at one of the royal pyramids."

"So what are you doing here then?"

"I want to bequeath my assets."

The guard stopped frowning. "Your assets?" he repeated, lowering his spear. "In that case, you'd better follow me, sire, and talk to Supadupa."

"Who's she?"

"Our High Priestess."

He led them into the courtyard. A group of temple maidens was crowding round two officials, one of whom held a plan.

"Your Holiness," grovelled the guard. "This gent wants to make a bequest."

She turned. The High Priestess was taller than anyone else, with flowing black hair and huge eyes framed with sticky black kohl.*

"Sounds interesting. What has he got?"

"I've got a big boat," boasted Dad. "And a big valuable gem!"

"Oooh, goody. How kind. What a nice man you are."

Dad beamed, "If you'd just put it in writing?"

"Of course. I shall order one of my temple scribes to write you a nice thank-you scroll. You can leave your boat at the quay. But why don't you give me the gem now?"

* Women could work in temples – see page 61

Dad's jaw dropped open, "G-give you?"

Supadupa kept smiling. "Yes, please."

"Excuse me," said Ptoni softly. "My Dad only wants his Will done."

"To leave all his assets to *meeeee*?"

"Not you, no. *Me*!"

"Oh dear," Supadupa's lower lip quivered. Her eyes bulged. The maidens twittered. The officials were shuffling their feet.

"It won't take long," Dad protested.

"We haven't got long!" said the man with the plan. "And we've got a mighty big problem with this obelisk."

"I'll rent you my crewmen," Dad offered. "They're highly skilled with big statues."

"This one's *tooooo* big," sighed the High Priestess.

"It's much too big for Breezbloc to get into the courtyard." She glanced at the man clutching the plan.

"No one could do it," huffed Breezbloc.

"I could," said the younger official at his side, a small man with sharp darting eyes.

"What do *you* know?" sneered Breezbloc. "You're a tax man. All you can do is catch poor folk who haven't paid their taxes and force them to work in my slave gang."

"First time I've heard you complain."

Ptoni stared at the tax man. It was Ferrut!

And the last time he'd seen Ferrut, the rat-faced little man had been carrying scrolls for Grubbiflub, the Chief Collector of Taxes.

"So how would you do it?" growled Breezbloc. "Make the obelisk jump over the wall?"

"I'd build a ramp," said Ferrut, "with rubble brought from the quarry."

"Oh, yes. I'd like to see you!"

"Perhaps you will – if her Holiness gives her gracious permission."

Supadupa turned to her temple maidens. "Shall I?"

They whispered to one another.

"It's worth a try . . ."

"What else can we do . . . ?"

"But can we rely on a tax man . . . ?"

"Ferrut's quite right," Dad broke in. "A ramp is just what I would advise. If you've got enough slaves, there's no problem."

"And what do *you* know?" challenged Breezbloc.

"He must know something about it. He says he's sorted out problems for Pharaoh at one of his pyramids," put in the guard with a sly wink at Ptoni.

"In that case," said Supadupa, looking confused but delighted, "he's somebody we can rely on. Perhaps he'd be kind and help Ferrut."

"On your heads be it!" roared Breezbloc.

"Or off with 'em, more likely, when Pharaoh sees the mess!" With that he stomped out of the courtyard.

"Sulky!" said Supadupa. "But don't take any notice of him. Succeed, and you'll be richly rewarded."

"You'll be covered in gold," cooed a maiden.

Dad whistled. "From head to toe? Both of us? Or just me?"

Ferrut peered at Dad more closely. "I've seen you somewhere before."

"Up his pyramid?" quipped the guard.

Ferrut raised his eyebrows. "Is that where your 'little gem' came from?"

"It's not so little," Dad beamed with pride. "My gem's an antique. It's enormous. You come to my boat and I'll show you. Then we can have a nice chat about our plans for this ramp. And what we can do with all the gold I'm going to get covered in."

"How could I refuse," Ferrut showed his sharp teeth. "I might bring a friend along too."

As soon as Ferrut had stalked off, Ptoni tried to remind Dad how dangerous the tax man might be.

"He's not collecting taxes now. What harm can he do to us? Oh look over there," said Dad. "It's poor old Breezbloc. Let's go and cheer him up."

Breezbloc had been hanging about behind the obelisk. He gave them a nasty scowl.

"What's that in your hand?" asked Dad. "It looks a bit sticky to me."

"So what?" Breezbloc closed his fist, but Dad prised his fingers open, revealing a big dollop of tar.

"I know that game," exclaimed Dad. "I played it when I was young. You coat a pebble in tar, then take it in turns to chuck it at something flat like that stone, and you win if you get it to stick."

An incredulous grin lit up Breezbloc's flat face. "That's right. Why don't you have first go? Just aim at the base of the obelisk."

Dad scored a hit first time. The tar-coated pebble stuck fast. He grinned with pride. "That shows how lucky I am."

Ptoni wasn't so sure. Looking away from Breezbloc, he noticed a large sleek galley had drawn up beside *Hefijuti*. He had a horrible feeling he knew who that galley belonged to.

Sure enough, when they reached the quay, he caught sight of Grubbiflub, the Chief Collector of Taxes, leaning over the side of their boat.

"Congratulations!" called Grubbiflub, as Dad hurried up the plank. "I hear from my old friend, Ferrut, that you have become the proud owner of a large precious gem. You must be a wealthy man."

"Oh no, not really," Dad burbled. "I mean, it's quite a small amethyst. I mean, it's so small that I've . . . er . . . lost it!"

"My guards will soon find it for you."

"But my boat's such a mess, please don't bother."

"It's got to be tidied," said Grubbiflub, giving a nod to the guards. "I need your boat to house my men during the Feast of Opet."

Dad stared at him in disbelief. "But I need it myself."

"No, you don't. Not while you're helping Ferrut with this obelisk.

You and your crewmen can sleep in the camp – along with the other slaves."

"Slaves? Sire, you don't understand –"

"I don't think I need to," said Grubbiflub beaming as one of the guards brought him the gem. "Now we're quits. This makes up for some of the taxes you haven't paid to Pharaoh over the years."

Dad stared in dismay. "But my son and my crew will starve."

"Not while I need them," grinned Ferrut. "They'll be well-fed – *if* they work hard."

"But what about me?" asked Dad.

"You offered to help, so naturally you'll be joining my work gang too." *

* Building a temple was hard work – see page 62

CHAPTER 4
WHO'S IN CHARGE?

They had to sleep in the camp that night, stretched out on hard, bumpy ground, with four or five hundred others. And long before dawn, they were made to get up by guards blowing trumpets in their ears.

"Come on, you slobs, time for breakfast. Then you can start shifting rubble."

"I'm not a donkey," Dad grumbled. "I was designed to do brain work."

"If you're so clever," said one of the lads, "you ought to be able to think up some crafty way of skiving off, chief."

"That's true," said Dad, and went quiet.

"At least the beer'th good," said Stupor.

It had an amazing effect. As they were passing the obelisk, Stupor managed to read out loud everything Skratch had engraved.

"Thith obelithk ith erected
By Pharaoh Armenlegup,
Whose lands are rich and coffers full
His subjects never fed up.

He's wise and yet so Fearful
His foes fall down and grovel,
Wild beasts retreat or they're dead meat
And –"

"Carry on," shouted the lads.

"I can't. That'th it," said Stupor.

"It hasn't been finished," said Dad. "Come on, Ptoni, you can do it. We need something to rhyme with grovel."

"Hovel?"

Dad drew in his breath, "That's not suitable for royalty."

"The beasts might hide a hovel," said one of the lads.

"Or Pharaoh's wives," added another. "They'd want to hide from Queen Mudpat."

"Stop mocking our Royals," snapped Ferrut, arriving on the scene to give them all their orders. "I'm sending half of you lot to fill your baskets with rubble – the rest form a line. Then I want you to pass the baskets from hand to hand down the line as far as the wall of the temple."

Dad put up his hand, "I'll help you to make sure they work hard, Ferrut."

"*You'll* work hard," shouted Ferrut, "or else you'll get beaten, you vile slave."

The sun came up. It got hot.

And then it got even hotter.

Still everyone carried on slaving, getting more and more sweaty, and more and more sticky with grime.

The heap of rubble by the jetty got smaller.

The heap of rubble by the temple got bigger.

It started to look like a ramp.

At midday they stopped for lunch and everybody collapsed – except for poor old Stupor, who'd gone to sleep on his feet.

But then Supadupa appeared with her maidens on top of the wall. "You can't let them stop," she told Ferrut. "We've just heard terrible news. Pharaoh is bringing Queen Mudpat!"

"Queen Mudpat?"

There were groans from the workforce. They all knew Pharaoh's senior wife was much more Fearful than he was!

Skratch cleared his throat: "Your Holiness, I'm sorry, but there's a slight problem."

"What with?"

"The bottom line."

"The bottom line," cried Ferrut, "is getting this job done on time."

"No, I mean the bottom line to go on the obelisk. I can't leave Pharaoh's inscription without a last line or Queen Mudpat might –"

"Might cut off your head," nodded Dad.

"So make something up," said the High Priestess. "I'm sure Pharaoh'll be pleased – if Queen Mudpat likes it."

"But what if she doesn't?" asked Skratch, rubbing his neck. "I can't risk it."

"In that case, leave it blank, but have some suggestions ready, so the Queen can choose," she said sweetly. "Remember it has to follow on from . . .

Wild beasts retreat or they're dead meat
And –"

"The Queen chomps 'em up," suggested a guard, making the maidens giggle.

"I don't think that rhymes," said Dad.

"How true," said Supadupa. "It's got to be really poetic. Any ideas, anybody? There must be a poet here somewhere?"

"Your Holiness," Dad put in, "my son is a natural poet. Why only this morning he told me something that rhymed with grovel. If you could kindly excuse us from this back-breaking toil and fetch us a nice cold drink – I'm sure we could find the right words!"

"You can't read or write," scoffed Ferrut.

"That's why I employ a personal scribe." Dad jabbed Stupor hard in the ribs, "Isn't that true? Come on, tell them!"

Instead of speaking, the old scribe stumbled sideways, letting his basket tilt over. A large lump of rock rolled out and crashed down on Ferrut's left foot.

"Yow-ow!" Ferrut hopped and hobbled. "My big toe – it's bleeding!"

"How icky," Supadupa covered her eyes. "I can't stand blood. Someone take him away."

"No problem," cried Dad. "My crewmen will carry poor old Ferrut to a doctor."

"But who'll be in charge here?" asked the High Priestess. "We need someone to give the slaves their orders."

The guard gave an evil chuckle. "What about him?" He pointed at Dad. "*He* was the one who gave the orders for building a pyramid, right?"

Lifting her hands from her eyes, Supadupa blinked so hard she made her eyelashes click. "Of course, our pyramid builder!"

CHAPTER 6
DAD'S BIG CHALLENGE

The news of Queen Mudpat's forthcoming visit spread quickly. Dad didn't need to say much to make the slaves work extra hard. By sunset the ramp was complete, sloping up to the wall of the temple.

"So who needs Ferrut?" Dad chuckled, while they were munching their supper. "It's me who'll get all the gold now!"

"If we get the obelisk up, Dad."

"We will. I'll be giving the orders."

"But what will the orders be, Dad?"

"I'll tell the slaves to just carry on . . . getting the obelisk up."

"How will they get it up?"

"I'll tell you," said Skratch, "if you promise to give me a share of the gold."

"Pah, what do *you* know?" Dad demanded.

"Well, as it so happens, my Grandad worked on the obelisk for King Milksop."

"So?"

Skratch drew a plan in the sand. "The obelisk goes up the ramp, over the top, facing backwards." Then he added a second ramp on the opposite side of the wall, sloping down into the courtyard. "Now, here's the trick." Skratch drew two more lines, curving down from the inner ramp, a third of the way along. "It goes down into this chimney which you build out of mud bricks. And as the obelisk goes down, its base slips into the chimney. Then it slides down, tilting upwards until it's on top of its plinth!"

Dad looked suspicious. "I wonder if it's
that easy. We had to shift a sphinx once, and
we got a chip on its shoulder just getting it out
of the boat. If this obelisk gets damaged, we're
done for."

"It won't," said Skratch, "and I'll show you why, but not until we reach that stage. I get half the gold, remember?"

Next morning they woke up tired and stiff, but the guards got them all back to work. They shifted another mountain of dirt. They must have lugged a thousand bricks.

And then they built the second ramp with the hollow chimney inside it.

"Now what do we do next, Skratch?" asked Dad.

"We fill the chimney with sand."

So the slaves filled the chimney with sand.

By mid-afternoon they were ready to harness the obelisk with dozens of strong, thick ropes.

Then everyone pulled or pushed except for Dad. And Stupor.

And as the sun was going down, bright red over the Nile, they managed to get the obelisk balanced on top of the wall.

"Heave!"

It slid over the top, down the opposite slope of the ramp, and into the mouth of the chimney. And that's where it stopped, with its base in the hole and the rest of it jutting out like an enormous finger pointing towards the sun.

Dad glanced at Skratch. "Now what?"

"Half," demanded Skratch.

"Don't be silly. I'll give you the gold from my toes to my knees. That's as far as I'll go," said Dad.

Skratch shook his head.

"Come on, that's quite generous."

"Up to your waist."

"I might stretch to my hips."

"*HALF*!"

"Oh, have it your own way."

"Right," Skratch got to his feet. "You remove some bricks from the bottom of the chimney and shovel out the sand."

It worked!

As the sand was removed, the obelisk slid slowly down, tilting up in the air until it was standing upright. Then everyone cheered.

"HURRAH!"

And Dad gave a modest bow. "I'm good at this, aren't I, Ptoni?"

"But aren't you forgetting one thing, Dad?"

"Removing the rubble? Don't worry. We've still got tomorrow morning and many slaves make light work."

"No, something else."

"Moving all the mud bricks?"

"No, Dad. The last line of the poem!"

"I've been rather busy here, Ptoni. I thought I could leave that to you."

"Why me?"

"Because you're the poet."

Ptoni was too tired to answer. And he was even more tired by the time all the rubble was cleared up late the following morning. Sitting down on a stack of mud bricks he started to worry again. But before he had any ideas there was a shout from the rooftops.

"Pharaoh's barge has been sighted. Queen Mudpat's on board. Action stations!"

As the last few slaves hurried off with their brooms, the temple maidens rushed in to empty baskets of petals over the newly-swept courtyard.

Then Pharaoh's guards streamed in.

Chief Counsellor Donut came next, followed by Grubbiflub on his mobile throne, with Ferrut behind on a stretcher.

Then Pharaoh's twenty-eight junior wives.

Then Prince Pitterpat, the King's-Eldest-Son-Of-His-Body, with his young wife, Anubit.

And finally, the Fearful Pharaoh was carried in on a huge throne. Queen Mudpat sat at his side, wearing a scary headdress.

Trumpets blared and cymbals crashed.

The temple maidens began a chant in honour of Amen-Ra.

Supadupa emerged from the temple carrying a large scroll. She started to sing in a high sweet voice about Pharaoh's obelisk being blessed by the gods.

But Queen Mudpat soon stopped her by clapping her hands. "Utter tosh! What's that

inscribed on its side? Read it out
loud, Donut."

Donut peered at the hieroglyphics and
recited clearly,

"This obelisk is erected
By Pharaoh Armenlegup,
Whose lands are rich and coffers full
His subjects never fed up.
He's wise and yet so Fearful
His foes fall down and grovel,
Wild beasts retreat or they're dead meat
And –"

"And?" demanded Queen Mudpat. "You mean there's more of this drivel?"

"Uh no, your Highness," said Donut.

"But even my Fearful husband knows that poems don't end with *and*!"

Pharaoh was twitching and tutting. "I made the poem up when I was in my bath. But when I got out it was time for bed. I must have forgotten to end it. Oh dearie me, what a nuisance."

"Humph," Queen Mudpat glared all around. "There must be somebody here in the crowd who can think up an end for this nonsense."

"Yes, ma'am," cried Dad. "We have here a highly-gifted young poet who has given the matter much thought. In fact, he's my son. Well, Ptoni?"

Ptoni's mind went blank.

And in the silence that followed he heard a faint *clickerty-click* and *clunk-clunk-clunk*.

"Whatever's that noise?" asked Pharaoh.

"It's your obelisk," muttered the Queen. "It's rocking about in the breeze. The fools haven't put it up properly. If you're so keen to be Fearful, you'd better start cutting some heads off."

Pharaoh's eyebrows wiggled, "Who first?"

"Ask who was in charge."

"Good idea. So who was in charge please?"

"Don't look at me, sire," gasped Breezbloc. "I'd never have put it up that way, but Ferrut was given my job, sire, so on his head be it, or off it – whatever's your pleasure, Your Highness."

"It's not my fault either, Your Highness," yelped Ferrut. "Alas, I was injured or I'd have ensured your obelisk stood like a rock for all time, sire. It was his fault!"

He pointed at Dad.

"Ptoni," gasped Dad. "Say something!"

Ptoni fell on his knees. He grasped the Fearful ankles. "Oh please, your Great Highness, my Dad tried his best. He did try terribly hard to get your obelisk right."

"*Tried?*" exclaimed Queen Mudpat. "Let me *try* and cut his silly head off. It might take four or five chops!"

"No, wait," Pharaoh put his hands up. "Just tell me why it's wobbling."

"Because you're so weak," snapped his wife. "That clown made it wobble on purpose."

Ptoni remembered the pebble that Breezbloc had covered in tar. Dad had chucked it so hard it had stuck – onto the base of the obelisk! It was making the obelisk wobble. That's how Breezbloc had got his revenge.

Now Dad was going to be beheaded. Unless . . .

Clickerty-click, *clunk-clickerty-clunk*.

"Give me your axe," the Queen bellowed.

A guard handed over his axe while the other guard forced Dad to his knees, so he was ready to get the chop. Supadupa covered her face with her hands and the obelisk swayed in the breeze.

Then, *click*. Ptoni suddenly got it. He knew what the last line of Pharaoh's poem could be.

It wasn't a good rhyme but (*clickerty-click*) it might be better than nothing so (*clunk-clickerty-click*) scrambling back onto his feet he cried, "Dad did it on purpose because –"

"You see, I knew it was sabotage," shouted the Queen, raising the axe in both hands.

"No, no, Dad only did it to make the obelisk more unusual, so people will come to see it, and read this special last line of the poem. It proves that we really wanted to make Pharaoh seem *extra* Fearful."

He stopped for breath and mopped his brow. Then in a slow measured voice, Ptoni began to recite,

"He's wise and yet so Fearful
His foes fall down and grovel,
Wild beasts retreat or they're dead meat
*And – **even his obelisk wobbles**."*

Silence.

Pharaoh frowned so hard his eyebrows started to wobble. The Queen's many chins started wobbling. The axe in her hand started wobbling. She turned away but she couldn't hold back a splutter. It sounded like a blocked drain. Then everyone heard her titter.

Donut cleared his throat and couldn't hold back a small giggle.

Pitterpat let out a chuckle.

Grubbiflub chortled out loud.

And soon everyone was laughing so much, the courtyard was rocking and rolling.

But Pharaoh carried on frowning, until the noise finally faded. "Why didn't *I* think of that last bit, about my obelisk wobbling?"

"You couldn't have, sire," said Dad quickly, "because you weren't to know that I would make your obelisk wobbly."

Pharaoh thought about this. "Of course not," he said. "Stands to reason."

"But it was the rest of your poem that really inspired us," said Ptoni.

Then Pharaoh twitched a small smile. And raising one finger he sang this song, dancing a little jig,

"The Great Sun God Ra
Is a super star
Spinning round
On his solar disc
But thanks to this boy
My heart fills with joy
Because there's no longer a risk
I won't fade away
For my name's here to stay
On my very own obelisk."
Then everyone clapped politely.
"Oh, very good, sire," beamed Donut.
"How shall we reward the boy?"

"A double reward,"
Dad put in
quickly.
"Perhaps
you could
cover us
both in
gold."

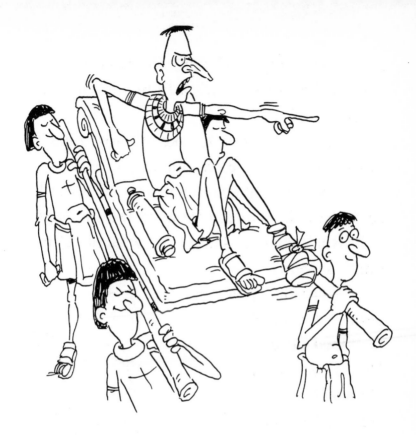

"What a cheek!" Ferrut cried from his stretcher. "Your Highness, you can't reward them! We put them in the work gang. They'd not paid any taxes for years!"

"I think I'll forgive them," said Pharaoh. "Let that be the end of the matter."

"But please, sire," Dad put his hand up. "They've got to give us our boat back."

"You surely don't think I'd want it?" scoffed Grubbiflub. "It's a filthy old tub. You can have it."

"You could use it to take all those mud bricks away," suggested Supadupa.

"And you can keep them as your reward," said Pharaoh, clapping Ptoni on the shoulders.

"But hang on," said Dad, "what about my precious gem?"

"Your son's precious gem of a last line will be inscribed in stone," declared Donut, "and people will come and read it for generations to come!"

"So I'll be remembered for thousands of years. Forever!" cried Pharaoh. "Now everyone sing." He threw back his head and warbled,

My heart fills with joy
Because there's no longer a risk . . ."

"All together," roared Donut. And as he lifted his voice in song, the crowd joined in,

"No he won't fade away
For his name's here to stay –

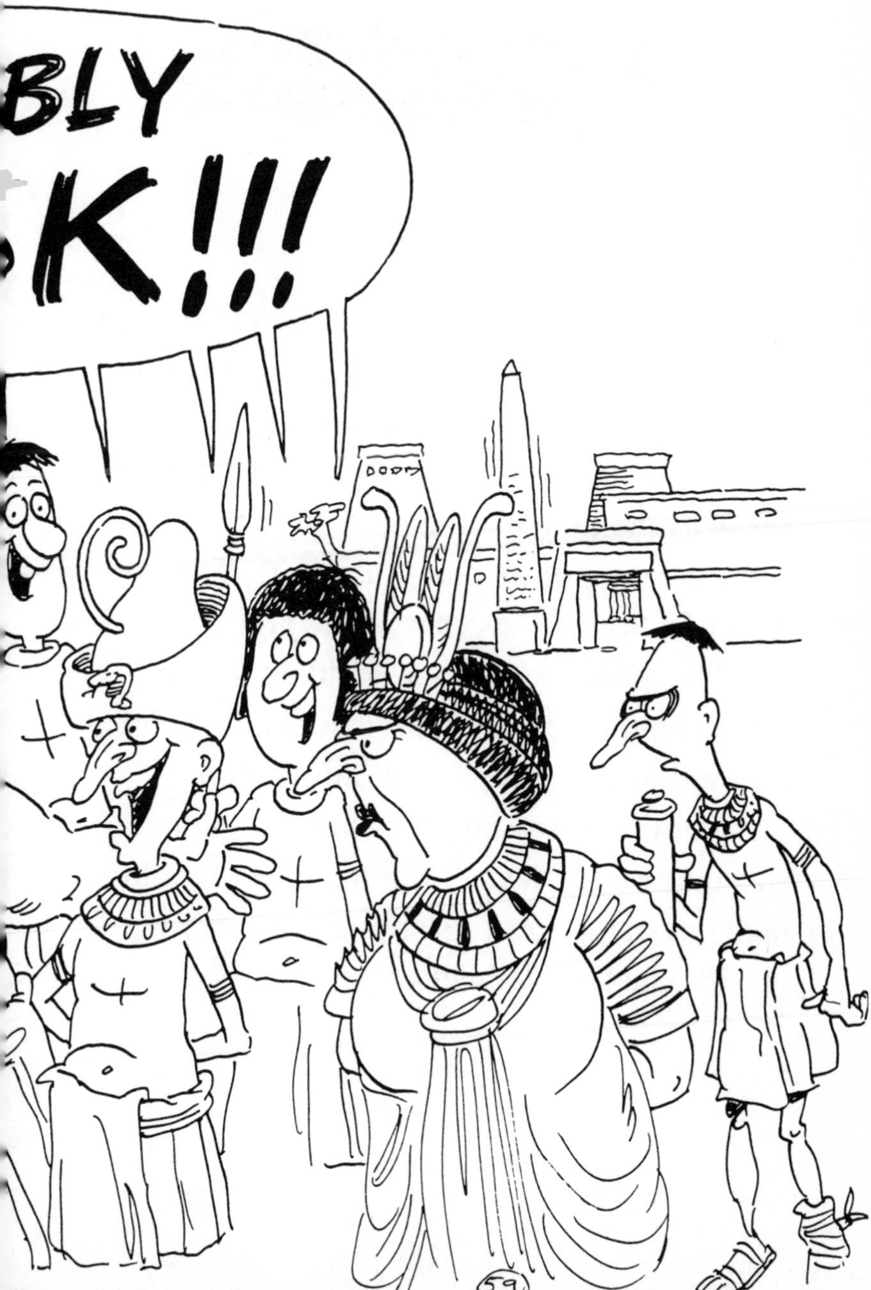
BLY
K!!!

NILE FILE-O-FACTS

Temples

Each Egyptian temple was dedicated to one of the gods or goddesses. It contained a shrine where an image of the god was kept in the form of a statue. The temple's purpose was to serve as the god's home on earth where he was cared for by priests and priestesses. Their official title was 'servant of the god'.

The temple was not a building where worshippers met. Ordinary people were not allowed to go in at all, but only got an opportunity to see and worship the statue on special festival days. Then the priest would take the statue from its shrine and carry it outside the temple walls.

Priestesses

Egyptian women played an important role in religion. Many well-born ladies were priestesses who sang the responses during prayers. Less well-born women performed as dancers to entertain the god. During ceremonies, they also played stringed instruments and shook tambourines and rattles.

Building temples

Like many ancient buildings, Egyptian temples were not built once and then left. They were continually extended and renewed by construction gangs. The work was strenuous and dangerous. Workers toiled in the burning sun with only simple equipment to help them. The working week in Ancient Egypt lasted nine days – the tenth being a day of rest. Workers were free to go home to their families if the distance was not too great.